D0455466

A Note to Parents and Caregivers:

Read-it! Readers are for children who are just starting on the amazing road to reading. These beautiful books support both the acquisition of reading skills and the love of books.

 The PURPLE LEVEL presents basic topics and objects using high frequency words and simple language patterns.

 The RED LEVEL presents familiar topics using common words and repeating sentence patterns.

 The BLUE LEVEL presents new ideas using a larger vocabulary and varied sentence structure.

 The YELLOW LEVEL presents more challenging ideas, a broad vocabulary, and wide variety in sentence structure.

 The GREEN LEVEL presents more complex ideas, an extended vocabulary range, and expanded language structures.

 The ORANGE LEVEL presents a wide range of ideas and concepts using challenging vocabulary and complex language structures.

When sharing a book with your child, read in short stretches, pausing often to talk about the pictures. Have your child turn the pages and point to the pictures and familiar words. And be sure to reread favorite stories or parts of stories.

There is no right or wrong way to share books with children. Find time to read with your child, and pass on the legacy of literacy.

Adria F. Klein, Ph.D.
Professor Emeritus
California State University
San Bernardino, California

Editor: Jill Kalz
Designer: Amy Muehlenhardt
Page Production: Angela Kilmer
Art Director: Nathan Gassman
Associate Managing Editor: Christianne Jones
The illustrations in this book were created with watercolor and pencil.

Picture Window Books
151 Good Counsel Drive
P.O. Box 669
Mankato, MN 56002-0669
877-845-8392
www.capstonepub.com

Printed in the United States of America in Stevens Point, Wisconsin.
022010
005697R

All books published by Picture Window Books
are manufactured with paper containing at least
10 percent post-consumer waste.

Library of Congress Cataloging-in-Publication Data
Klein, Adria F. (Adria Fay), 1947–
Max celebrates Chinese New Year / by Adria F. Klein ; illustrated by
Mernie Gallagher-Cole.
p. cm. — (Read-it! readers. The life of Max)
Summary: Max's friend Lily invites him to her family's celebration of
Chinese New Year.
ISBN-13: 978-1-4048-3147-6 (library binding)
ISBN-10: 1-4048-3147-9 (library binding)
ISBN-13: 978-1-4048-3287-9 (paperback)
ISBN-10: 1-4048-3287-4 (paperback)
[1. Chinese New Year—Fiction. 2. Friendship—Fiction. 3. Hispanic Americans—
Fiction.] I. Gallagher-Cole, Mernie, ill. II. Title.
PZ7.K678324Mac 2006.
[E]—dc22   2006027296

Max Celebrates Chinese New Year

by Adria F. Klein
illustrated by Mernie Gallagher-Cole

Special thanks to our advisers for their expertise:

Adria F. Klein, Ph.D.
Professor Emeritus, California State University
San Bernardino, California

Susan Kesselring, M.A.
Literacy Educator
Rosemount–Apple Valley–Eagan (Minnesota) School District

PiCTURE WiNDOW BOOKS
Minneapolis, Minnesota

Max and Lily are good friends.

Lily invites Max to a party with her family. Tomorrow is the first day of the Chinese New Year.

7

Lily is very excited. She tells Max that the Chinese New Year is like the New Year's Day he celebrates.

Max celebrates on January 1.

The Chinese New Year takes place in January or February. It lasts fifteen days. Lily's family celebrates each day in special ways.

Lily and her parents get ready for the party. They clean the house.

Max helps them.

Lily and Max put a red cloth on the dinner table.

Red is for good luck.

Lily puts flowers on the table. Flowers are for happiness.

Max puts oranges on the table.

Oranges, too, are for good luck.

The next day, Lily, her parents, and
Max wear new clothes for the Chinese
New Year.

They eat sweet rice. They eat cookies
and sweet candy, too.

Lily and Max have a lot of fun watching the dragon parade.

Max wants to celebrate the Chinese New Year with Lily every year.

Max and Lily are good friends.